M000209676

VACATION OF A LIFETIME

Roscoe Donaldson

COPYRIGHT © 2023 Roscoe Donaldson

No part of this publication may be reproduced, stored in a retrieval system, or transmitted, in any form or by any means, electronic, mechanical, photocopying, recording, or otherwise, without the express written permission of the author.

Printed by:
Amazon Book Publication

Printed in the United States of America

First Printing Edition, 2023
ISBN (to be inserted)

TABLE OF CONTENTS

DEDICATION

For my parents Donald and Harriet Ross.

Mom, thank you for supporting me in everything I ever did.

Dad, thank you for teaching me that you don't have to know everything, to attempt anything.

And, thank you both for giving me the best life I could ever ask for.

ACKNOWLEDGMENTS

I wish to thank my wife for believing in me, pushing me to write when I didn't want to and giving me the quiet time needed to complete this project, I couldn't and wouldn't have seen it through without you.

I wish to thank my Beta readers who kept asking for "more" but not too much! Debbie, Molly, Linda and Tim. All of your input is appreciated.

Thank you to my editor Rebecca, I appreciate your double checks.

Thank you to my blog followers who encouraged me to keep going!

And a big thank you to Mitch, Walt, Stephanie and Penny, characters who, if they did not exist, this story would never have been written.

ABOUT THE AUTHOR

Roscoe Donaldson was adopted when he was six months old and grew up in the small town of Concrete, Washington in the North Cascades.

Roscoe now lives on the Washington coast with his wife. They have three adult children and two cats.

When he is not writing, Roscoe can be found spending his free time either walking on the beach with his bride, geocaching, working in the flower beds and greenhouse or some task involving nature, and coming up with ideas for his next story.

PROLOGUE

The small plane dipped lower as it approached the open-air eating area above the beach immediately attracting the attention of the diners. Everyone stood up and gathered at the railing overlooking the rocky cliffs and smooth brown sand below.

The plane dipped toward the water and then shot straight up, disappearing into the low cloud cover. Suddenly the sound of a plane engine filled the dining area as the pilot maneuvered the small plane at an angle to the dining area, skillfully banked so that the bottom of the plane faced the diners, a colorful smoke spewed from the back of the plane followed by a banner saying "Welcome to Mazatlan!"

The crowd all gave a resounding applause and many cheered at the excitement of the unplanned air show.

The diners, however, were clueless as to what was really happening until it was too late. While they were all watching the trick plane, four small drones made their way into and through the open-air restaurant.

The first drone caused a small explosion resulting in a small fire breaking out in the main dining area. The flames from this fire immediately activated the fire suppression system, but due to the amount of accelerant carried on this drone, the system was not sufficient enough to douse the flames.

As it turned out, three of the drones were equipped with explosive devices, while the fourth exited the building as quickly as it had entered, and casually hovered over the building.

Again, if anyone had had the chance to be observant, they would have seen the two small missiles fly directly into the chaos and effortlessly explode, ensuring total destruction of the building and its occupants.

ROSCOE DONALDSON

Vacation of a Lifetime

CHAPTER ONE

SUMMER, 1974

"Ok honey, have a great time, see you in a couple hours." Mitch's mom said to him. Mitch looked at his mom from the passenger seat of their Chrysler Brougham, shifted a little to the side, looked down at the floorboard of the car and said, "But mom, what if no one likes me?"

"Mitchell Scott!" she said, "everyone is going to like you, and you may even meet new friends" Mitch knew when his mom used his middle name, she meant business.

"I doubt it," said Mitch as he reluctantly pulled open the passenger door, reached in to grab his swimsuit and towel that were perfectly rolled up, shoved them under his arm and shuffled his feet through the gravel parking lot, getting rocks inside his flip flops. He paused, shook out his footwear and continued his trek to the outdoor pool.

The smell of chlorine mixed with sunscreen filled the air. Sounds of water lapping against the cement sides of the pool, along with the twang of the diving board springs could be heard as the cyclone fence gate closed with a sharp metallic tone as the bracket slid down the pole. A lifeguard blew their shrill whistle and pointed to a pair of young men who were horse playing and dunking each other as a warning against their actions. The whistle sounded again, and the lifeguard yelled at some of the new arrivals "No running! We don't need anyone slipping and cracking their head open!"

Mitch reluctantly walked down the tiled ramp to the boys' locker room, it always seemed a little dark in there compared to the bright sunshine outside but his eyes quickly adjusted. Someone had left the last shower running, and you couldn't get to the changing area without having to walk through it. Mitch was irritated that someone would do that, but it was all part of having a public swimming pool. He dodged the spray as best as he could, of course the temperature was set all the way to hot, so anyone attempting to turn off the faucet would risk a quick scalding.

Mitch made his way to the wooden benches in the middle of the changing room, there were door less lockers where a few brave souls actually left their personal belongings, but from past experience, most swimmers shoved any valuables in their shoes, or their swim bags and toted them to the deck chairs surrounding the pool, there they would stand a better chance of not being stolen. Mitch quickly stripped off his gym shorts and underwear, slipped on his bathing trunks, pulled off his shirt and neatly rolled them back into the towel where his trunks had previously been. Leaving his roll on the wooden bench, Mitch walked back into the shower area, dodged the hot shower that had been left on, changed the temperature to a more manageable zone and rinsed himself off. He then returned to the bench, grabbed his belongings and ascended back up the ramp to the pool area.

Mitch quickly put his free hand over his eyes to shade him from the bright light. He looked over to the right, and saw an empty chair where he could place his belongings. He slipped off his flip-flops under the chair and placed his toweled bundle on the chair. Hopefully it would be enough to keep the $2.00 he had in his gym shorts safe. His mother had given him the two one-dollar bills in case of an emergency, like needing a coke or a snow cone during her absence.

Mitch went to the side of the pool, trying to decide if he wanted to jump in, or use the ladder to slowly enter the frigid water. Deciding to jump, he held his nose and jumped straight out into the deep end of the water. Mitch was an excellent swimmer, having taken swimming lessons from a young age, and he felt at home in and under the water as much as he did walking on the dry land. He opened his eyes once he was under the water, sounds of delightful screaming, and even the diving board were muffled under the water, he wondered if the sounds were similar to what whales heard.

Mitch kicked off the bottom of the pool, pulled his arms in a breaststroke fashion and swam underwater to the shallow end of the pool. He was able to stand and rise from the water, as he did so, he wiped his eyes of the excess water and when he opened his eyes, another boy about his age was standing in front of him.

"Hi" said the other boy, "My name is Walter, but my friends call me Walt, what's yours?"

Mitch looked at him, almost the same height, Walt was a little skinnier than himself, not grossly thin, but obviously athletic. He had dark brown hair that was in a tousled mess from the water, and wore Bermuda short swim trunks, paling Mitch's boring blue swim trunks with the white string that tied in front.

"I'm Mitchell", he said, "but my friends call me Mitch"

"Nice to meet you Mitch," Walt said, indicating that they would be friends. "You are pretty good in the water, are you on the swimming team?" asked Walt.

"No, I thought about trying out, but never really pursued it" answered Mitch.

"Well, I think you should, try-outs are next week, and I will be there" said Walt.

"Yeah?" said Mitch. "I will ask my mom if I can try out as well"

"Think about it Mitch," said Walt. "We will be a force to be reckoned with at the state tournament"

CHAPTER TWO

FRIENDLY COMPETITION

From that day forward, Mitch and Walt were best friends. They spent most of their weekends together swimming and training during the season, or hiking, playing soccer and other physical activities throughout the rest of the year.

The two friends were so closely matched in their swimming skills that they were often forced to compete with each other. When the city they lived in decided to enclose the public pool it was a perfect opportunity for the school to ramp up their swimming teams' activities. With an indoor pool they could train and swim year round, not just during the summer.

The whistle blew and Mitch launched himself off the podium, hitting the water with much more majestic style than the week before. This was one event when he was competing against his best friend Walt, as he turned his head to the side and gulped a breath between freestyle arm pulls, he saw Walt in the lane next to him seemingly swimming at the same pace as his friend. They reached the wall at almost the same moment, flipped their bodies over under water and kicked off at the same rate of speed. Coming to the surface, Mitch looked over and could not see Walt, had he beaten him off of the wall? Setting his sights forward again, he began to pull with all his might. Suddenly about 2 feet in front of him he saw a head surface in the lane beside him. Walt had had a stronger kick-off on the wall this time and he saw his friend begin his long freestyle strokes. He knew that second place would have to be good enough today.

By the time he reached the finish line, Walt was pulling himself out of the water. He rejected someone's offer of a towel and quickly made his way over to the next lane, reaching down and grasping his best friend's hand, helping him pull himself out of the water. The two young men embraced as best friends and competitors do.

Walt shouted "You almost had me on that one! You are really improving, just wait until we get older and take tropical vacations, your swimming skills will slay the ladies!"

Cameras flashed, people cheered and there was a very nice write-up on the meet in the local paper the next day."

They both qualified for the state tournament their senior year in college and were very excited, until they learned they would be swimming the final event against each other.

CHAPTER THREE

STATE TOURNAMENT, MITCH AND WALT'S SENIOR YEAR IN COLLEGE

Walt and Mitch both competed very well in the state tournament, both young men placed first in their respective heats and their anxiety levels grew as they prepared for the final event.

Mitch took to the podium for the final event. This was a medley heat that included freestyle, breaststroke and concluded with the butterfly. Mitch looked two lanes over and saw his friend Walt. Swimming cap and goggles on, Walt stood with his arms angled behind him, torso leaning slightly forward waiting for the starting whistle. Mitch looked towards the crowd and noticed this attractive blonde sitting on the edge of her seat, by herself in the stands. Mitch took a deep breath, positioned his body in a similar fashion to Walt's and waited a few seconds until the sound of the starting whistle. Both men flung themselves into the water at precisely the same speed and accuracy.

The heat was so closely matched that the timekeepers were forced to keep their eyes on their stopwatches and depend on the spotters in the lanes to mark their kick off times rather than watching the swimmers.

Mitch flipped his feet over his head during the final lap of the butterfly portion of the heat. He misjudged the distance needed and his feet connected not with water, pushing him to the final lap and victory, but instead landing on hard concrete. The impact of hitting both his feet on the edge of the Olympic sized pool caused several bones in both feet to break, although the skin stayed intact the pain was so severe that he blacked out for a moment and started sinking. There was a small splash as the blonde had come running to the edge of the pool, pulled off her swim cover-up revealing a lifeguard swimsuit and gracefully dived into the water. The blonde grasped Mitch around the neck in a lifesaving hold and kicked forcefully to the surface, once above the water, she kept an arm securely around his head allowing air to enter through his nose and open mouth. Mitch sputtered a bit, coughed on pool water but still remained unconscious. The blonde lifeguard used her powerful legs and other arm to push them both to the side of the pool where Walt and others stood waiting to haul him out of the water.

Once they had Mitch safely on the hard concrete deck, Walt glanced over to his girlfriend Penny, both with almost identical panicked looks. Penny raced out of the stands and joined Walt, and the small crowd that had gathered. They all stepped back, as the lifeguard checked to see if Mitch was breathing, and noticing he was not, she began doing

CPR. After the second round of chest compressions, she began to give him breaths, she turned his head to the side, he expelled some water and his eyes fluttered open.

The blonde looked him in the eyes and said "you really had us worried for a minute there."

Mitch said "Oh my God! Thank you, to whom do I owe my gratitude?"

The blonde looked back at him and said "my name is Stephanie, and you owe me dinner and a drink once you get out of the hospital."

Mitch said, "Why would I go to the hospital? You saved me!" Suddenly the pain from his broken feet came roaring through the rest of his senses and he remembered why he would be going to the hospital.

CHAPTER FOUR

RECOVERY

As the doors to the ambulance closed, Penny and Walt looked back to the grandstand area and saw Stephanie sitting by herself looking worried.

Penny took Walt's' hand and led him to where Stephanie was sitting. Penny extended her hand "I'm Penny, this is my boyfriend Walter" she said as Stephanie grasped her hand in response and gave it a firm shake. "We wanted to thank you for saving our friend's life!"

"My friends call me Walt" Walt said and extended his hand, when Stephanie accepted his hand, he brought her in for a tight embrace and used his other arm to draw Penny into a three-person hug. "I was really worried, I am so glad you were here." Walt said.

"It is nice to meet you both," Stephanie said. "Penny and....Walt, I am sure we will see each other again. I am starting work at the aquatic center next week. Today was my first observation day."

"Hell of a first day," said Walt. "We are going to go to the hospital and check up on our friend, you are welcome to join us if you like."

Stephanie nodded and said "I would like that"

As Walt emerged from the locker room. He spied Penny and Stephanie sitting in the now vacant grandstands. They both stood as he approached them. Stephanie had changed out of her lifeguard swimsuit and wore a pair of light-colored pants and a button-up top.

"Ready?" Walt asked Penny.

"Yes, and Stephanie is going to follow us in her car" Penny replied.

❀❀❀

The trio got to the hospital just as the doctors finished casting Mitch's feet.

"Hey man" said Walt with a grin on his face, "If you hadn't of thrown the race, you may have actually beaten me this time."

"Well, all I can say is it was too close to call, next time!" answered Mitch.

The doctor said, "You are going to be in a wheelchair for at least the next two weeks, and then if you behave you can graduate up to walking casts, is there anyone that can help you out during this time?"

"Yeah, I'll stay with my mom for a couple weeks"

Stephanie said "I can come help after my shift at the aquatic center" She lowered her eyes and said "if you want".

Mitch said "that would be great, and it would help out my mom as well"

Stephanie said "Let me see your phone"

Mitch dug into his bag and handed her his phone, Stephanie punched her number in and stored it for him. "Call me tomorrow, once I have my schedule I can make some plans with your mom."

Two weeks seemed to fly by, other than the minimal pain Mitch experienced, his recovery went very well thanks to his two dedicated nurses. Stephanie and Mitch's mom became good friends and shared laughs over stories of Mitch growing up and his experience with swimming.

Once the two weeks had passed, Mitch and Stephanie were officially an item. His dreams of a career in professional swimming and enlisting into the Navy SEALs had literally been broken.

Stephanie encouraged him that even though he would not be able to swim professionally, he could still swim! Mitch decided to enroll in the appropriate training and soon was certified as a lifeguard, he and Stephanie spent most of their days together either working poolside or spending their shared days off in the park, having picnic lunches or romantic dinners.

During his recovery period, Mitch decided he should have something to fall back on in the event he could not swim again so he enrolled in online classes to get his Certified Public Accountant license. It turned out that the only thing he was better at than swimming was crunching numbers and doing tax returns.

CHAPTER FIVE

WALTER AND PENNY

"C'mon son, you got this!" Walt's dad yelled from the sidelines of the soccer field.

Young Walt increased his gait as he chased the black and white ball down the field. His shorts were a little too big, and the white shirt he wore flapped in the breeze created by his speed. The cleats he wore were new that season, and he had not really had a chance to break them in so, his feet were a little sore but, because of his father's prompting, he still managed to squeak a little more speed out of himself.

Walt had always looked up to his dad, being elite naval personnel he was the best of the best in his field. He was a member of the Navy SEALs, often deployed overseas for months at a time helping to keep the peace.

Today was his dad's last day stateside for a while, as he was being deployed the next day for who knows how long.

Their family had moved around a lot because of his dad's occupation and had recently settled down in this small community about an hour and a half from the base where his dad was stationed.

Walt sped down the field, despite his sore feet, and managed to catch up to the opponents who were kicking the ball back and forth dribbling towards the goal. The taller of the two drew his foot back, kicked the black and white sphere firmly with the side of his foot towards the goal. The goalie jumped toward his left side, extended his arms and managed to block the goal.

The goalie then grasped the ball with both hands, raised his arms over his head and threw the ball as far as he could, over the two opponents' heads, directly in front of Walt. Walt watched the ball as it bounced in front of him, waited about half a second and slammed his new soccer shoe into it with all his might. The ball flew down the field, into a group of his teammates who then proceeded to move the ball towards their own goal.

Walt ran as fast as his feet would carry him towards the other end, an opposing teammate swung at the ball and connected with a portion of it, moving the ball a few feet back down the field and straight towards Walt. Walt ran straight at the ball that was coming at him, booted it as hard as he could. The ball took a slight curve to the right and caught the goalie off-guard. The goalie had been so involved in focusing on the other members of the team that he had not noticed Walt coming straight down the field. The ball whizzed by him, a mere 3 inches from his hands. Score!

The game came to an end, Walt's team had defeated the visitors by a score of 2-1.

"Let's celebrate!" said Walt's dad. As they drove towards the local drive-in for celebratory ice cream, Walt loosened the laces on his cleats and slipped them off. He pulled his sock off, and noticed the blister forming on the side of his foot due to not having properly broken his shoes in.

'Hey dad?" Walt asked, "Would you be too disappointed if I stuck to swimming"?

Walt's dad looked at his foot and said "You know, it might be better, at least you don't need shoes for swimming. In fact", he added "The town pool is set to open next week, you should have mom drop you off for open swim, maybe you could meet some new friends in the area, and be better prepared to head to school in the fall".

"Sounds good to me" his mother replied, "let's stop by the office on the way and pick up a schedule".

A few weeks later it was Independence day, Walt's new best friend Mitch was unavailable to attend family day with him, so Walt was a little bummed and hesitant about attending the event. Walt's mom was insistent that they go to the event so that they could spend time around other military families, and lean on them for support while their spouses were deployed.

As Walt sat at a picnic table looking at the crowd through the mirrored sunglasses his dad had given him before deployment, a woman used a megaphone to address the families.

"We will be having a series of short games for the kids starting in ten minutes" she called into the microphone. "The three legged race will be our first event".

"Great", thought Walt, if Mitch were here, we would crush this. Walt had met Mitch at the local pool during his first open swim after he abandoned his tight soccer cleats and decided to follow in his father's footsteps of spending his life in the water.

The woman announcing the games came over to his table and said "you want to enter the three-legged race"?

"I don't have anyone to race with," Walt answered, still a little bummed that his buddy couldn't come.

"Well, I can help with that, Penny honey, come over here a minute" a dark haired girl about Walt's age jogged over to the picnic table. "This is my daughter Penny, Penny, this is...." "I'm sorry, I didn't get your name"

"Walter, but my friends call me Walt," he said.

"Hello...Walter" Penny said, "I have a gunny sack and need an extra leg" she said.

Walt laughed and said "Ok, but try not to drag me down"

Penny smirked and said "YOU try not to drag ME down!"

The racers were beginning to line up on the white line that had been painted on the green grass. There was another line painted one hundred feet away. Walt and Penny were very close in height and made a good match for this type of race. The duo spent a few minutes practicing their strides and then made their way to the starting line. Walt put his arm around Penny's waist, and she did the same to him. The starting pistol sounded, and the pair began by stepping together with their connected feet.

Other racers who had not taken the time to take a few practice steps started with their opposing legs and quickly staggered, some fell to the damp earth, laughing while Walt and Penny trudged ahead, both determined to come out on top. They crossed the finish line a good 2 seconds before the nearest couple, they removed their arms from each other's waists, grasped hands, and fell to the ground, laughing, and gasping for air.

"Great job teammate!" said Penny.

"You too," said Walt. "How about the next event?" "We do pretty well together."

"Sounds good" answered Penny, "eggs on spoons".

Walt and Penny spent the rest of the afternoon together, they competed together in every couple's event, and cheered each other on in their individual events.

They talked, laughed, ate strawberry shortcake and watched the fireworks together.

"How long is your dad deployed?" asked Penny.

"I'm not sure, they don't have a return date yet." "How about yours?" Walt asked.

"Same story," answered Penny. "The squadron chief wasn't sure how long the mission would be" "Something overseas, trying to keep the peace with arms deals, that's all I know."

"You mean that's all they can tell you," said Walt. What squad is your dad in?

"SEAL team six," Penny said.

"No kidding?" answered Walt, "so is mine, crazy they are deployed together."

"It is a small world...Walt..." said Penny.

It was at this moment that the two of them knew they were destined to be together. Walt and Penny spent most of their time together, when they were not in school, they were hanging out together at the beach, having barbecues or going to the movies.

Walt was extremely proud when he introduced his best friend to his girlfriend.

Penny was always supportive of Walt and his swimming, and in turn supported Mitch as well. When Walt announced that after college he was planning on joining the SEALs like his father, it was assumed that Penny would become the family advocate for the squad and Mitch's swimming skills made him a natural to join Walt in their future.

❀❀❀

Years Later...

Walt looked at the recruiter and said "No, I changed my mind, since my buddy Mitch can't get in, I decided I don't want to be a SEAL. Not without Mitch."

The recruiter said, "Look Walter, you can still help your country out, you don't have to be a SEAL to do so."

"You've got me curious." Walt replied.

The recruiter said, "You can still utilize your knowledge and skills to help the country, we are looking for someone to work undercover to aid in our war on terrorism, would you be interested in that?"

Walt chewed on his lip as the recruiter explained what would be involved in the position, by the time he was done, he was sold on the idea.

"No one has to know? Not even my family and friends?" Water asked.

"We would rather they didn't." Answered the recruiter.

CHAPTER SIX

STEPHANIE

"Oh my god!" the woman screamed as she dropped the towel she was carrying. The towel landed in a small puddle of pool water and instantly becoming unusable. "He can't swim! Someone please help!" Her young boy had come running into the pool area from the changing room and immediately jumped feet first into the deep end of the Olympic size swimming pool.

Several bystanders gasped and began shouting at no one in particular, a man's voice boomed over the dull roar of the crowd shouted "where is the lifeguard?" A young blonde girl had just emerged from swimming underwater and heard the commotion. She looked towards the lifeguard chair, and saw it was unoccupied. She glanced in the other direction and saw the young boy slowly sinking towards the bottom of the ten foot pool. She hollered to the man who had shouted earlier "Grab that life ring and throw it in the water"!

Stephanie took a deep gulp of air and quickly submerged into the water, she used her strong arms and performed a huge underwater breaststroke as her feet pushed off the wall, towards the sinking boy. She reached the boy quickly and grasped him under the arms, pushed her feet off the floor of the pool, hard and began to ascend to the surface of the water.

They both broke through the water with a great splash. Stephanie took a breath of air, wrapped her left arm around the torso of the boy, brought her hand up to his chin keeping his face out of the water and used her free arm to propel them both through the water towards the floating life ring. She got to the ring, wrapped her free arm through the ring and shouted "PULL"!

The man began to pull on the yellow rope slowly dragging them towards the edge of the pool. Soon, another man grabbed the rope and doubled their efforts of towing them to the edge.

Once the duo had arrived at the edge of the pool, another person jumped into the pool and assisted Stephanie in getting the boy to the edge. The two men who had been pulling the rope reached down and hauled the boy onto the concrete deck. "He's not breathing"! One of the men shouted, the lifeguard who had come from the locker room quickly jumped into action.

"You there!" shouted the lifeguard, "Call 9-1-1" she told another bystander to go into the office and grab the first aid kit. The lifeguard tipped the young boy's head back, checked to see if he was breathing and started CPR.

Stephanie stood back, her long hair dripping down her body and her suit dripping added to the puddle of pool water that had ruined the poor boy's towel. She moved over to the child's mother, and grasped her hand as they all watched the lifeguard perform CPR compressions.

After the third round of compressions, the paramedics arrived, one medic looked at the lifeguard and said "well done, we will take it from here. "Everyone held their breath as the paramedic hooked up the defibrillator. The machine beeped and flashed a series of lights. After another round of compressions, the medic once again said "clear!" The charged paddles were placed on the child's chest area, after this shock the monitor sounded a series of beeps and the boys heart started beating again.

Stephanie grasped the mother's hand tighter as they both held their breaths. The paramedic turned the boy's head to the side as he expelled a portion of the pool water he had swallowed. The boy sputtered, took a deep breath and coughed. He opened his eyes, looked up at the paramedic and said "where's my mom?" His mother let out a loud sob of relief, released Stephanie's hand and knelt next to her boy. She cried and kissed his cheeks and forehead. "You scared me so much why did you jump into the water?"

"I was so excited, I just wanted to get in the water, I'm sorry mama" he sobbed.

The paramedics loaded the boy on a gurney. As they were about to close the doors, the mother looked over and said "Young lady, I don't know how to thank you. If it wasn't for you, my son would have drowned."

Stephanie picked up the sopping wet towel, wrung it out as best as she could and handed it to the mother. "I'm just glad it turned out the way it did, my name is Stephanie, and I hope this doesn't deter your son from swimming. They offer lessons here at the pool."

The boy looked up, "thank you Stephanie for everything and I will see you at the swimming lessons!" The paramedics closed the door with a bang, and Stephanie stood next to the lifeguard and watched until they turned the corner and drove out of sight.

The lifeguard looked at Stephanie and said "Thanks for your help, I am glad you were there, you saved his life with your quick thinking".

Stephanie took a ragged breath and said "I am glad too".

That day changed Stephanie's life. That was the day she decided she wanted to pursue a career in lifesaving. She loved the water and loved helping other people. "Are you hiring"? She asked the lifeguard.

"Come back next week and let's see what we can do," the lifeguard answered.

Stephanie began teaching swimming lessons and actually taught her biggest fan, the boy she had saved to become one of the best swimmers in the town. Not soon after, she received her official lifeguard accreditation and spent most of her days either in the water, or on the edge of it.

CHAPTER SEVEN

A VACATION IS PLANNED!

Mitch, Walt, Stephanie, and Penny had gathered at the local Mexican restaurant to celebrate the end of tax season. Mitch, a local CPA, and Walt an independent sales rep for aquatic equipment similar to scuba, and snorkeling supplies.

"What do you think about going to Mazatlan with us for a week?" asked Walt, while the festive music played a little too loud in the background. The sound of the blender at the bar added to the confusion and Mitch asked Walt to repeat himself to make sure he had heard correctly.

"Seven days in sunny Mazatlan. Sun, sand and relaxation. All the lodging is paid for. All you have to do is say yes." Walt said.

Mitch looked at his wife Stephanie who shot him an excited look and said "Oh Hell Yes!" even though his mouth was full of chips and salsa. "When?"

"Rude!" Stephanie said, elbowing her husband in the ribs. "We would love to join you, but we must insist on paying half of the lodging"

"We are thinking in May, that way tax season is over and you can take some time off, undisturbed," Walt answered. He glanced over to his wife Penny, scooped up some salsa on a chip and shoved it in his mouth. Walt continued "I could use the time to make some sales calls at the local resorts, tax write-off, right buddy?" he asked Mitch. "The only expenses you will have is airfare, food and any souvenirs you want. Like I said before the lodging is all covered under our annual plan, and it is use it or lose it situation."

Mitch laughed, and said "Yes, Walt, always looking for the tax break." The two couples laughed, ordered a fresh round of margaritas and began excitedly to make plans.

Seven days in a Mexican resort, *Sun, waves, pools, bars, shopping and relaxation. What could be bad about that?* Thought Mitch. One thing he decided was that he needed to brush up on his Spanish, he hadn't had a reason to speak the language since high school and other than remembering how to ask for 'papel de bano', or 'una mas cerveza, por favor', he felt he would be pretty lost.

CHAPTER EIGHT

ARRIVAL!

Mitch, Walt and their wives' anticipation of their vacation increased as the plane touched down at the Mazatlan airport.

It was a dry sunny day in Mexico and soon they were walking through the freshly mopped tiled hallway towards customs and the baggage claim area. The heat that blew through the hallway enhanced by the jet engines that idled just outside of the area was dry, almost dusty. Not as tropical as other places, but what could you expect from an airport in the desert, 11 miles from the resort town?

They quickly made their way through customs, showing their passports to the man behind the elevated counter. One big, rubber stamp showing their arrival date with a faded embossment of "Estados Unidos Mexico Arrival" and they were in Mexico. After they claimed their bags, they made a quick trip to the restroom, and the airport gift shop to grab a bottle of water, and they headed out into the heat to board the shuttle bus that would take them to the resort.

The air conditioning in the shuttle bus was only a slight refreshment from the dank outside air. They rumbled north for about 30 minutes. Although the main part of town was only about eleven miles from the airport, the roads were not in the best condition, and their resort was an additional two miles out of town.

They traveled along, squished into the small seats. Looking out at the dry, arid land, they noticed many cacti, a few iguanas, and smiled and waved at small groups of locals who stopped their work and took advantage of watching the tourists drive by to have a short break, and a drink of water.

Upon arriving at the resort, the shuttle driver pulled under the covered area at the front door of the main building. He quickly went to the back of the shuttle and began unloading baggage, as the hotel staff opened the side doors of the shuttle and began welcoming everyone to their destination.

Mitch, Stephanie, Walt and Penny gathered their luggage, went into the faintly air conditioned lobby and checked in. The floors of the lobby were freshly mopped, and they were beginning to notice a trend. The locals took great pride in their tiled floors, and attempted to keep them clean as a whistle. The foursome made their way to their room, and upon entering, noticed the same clean tile. Fortunately, Mitch thought the air conditioning worked much better in their room than it did in the lobby, shuttle van, or even the airport!

The couples unpacked their bags and got settled in their room. There would be lots of pool time, and touristy things to do in the next week, but for now, they mainly wanted to grab a bite to eat, maybe take a late night swim and call it a day.

They noticed a gift basket on the table, inside the basket was a small bottle of champagne and a business card with the number of a local pulmonia service which turned out is Spanish for an open air taxi, and a pamphlet of tours to consider while in Mazatlan.

They all slept really well that night, partly due to the day of traveling, but also the excitement of finally having begun the vacation they had planned and saved for, for so long.

At one point during the night, they noticed a shrill chirp traveling through the room. Thinking it was the smoke detector, both men checked them, and there were no issues. Once they settled back down, the chirp sounded again. Mitch and Walt gathered back in the kitchen area and waited to hear it again. When it did sound again, it was in one of the bedrooms.

Penny shrieked, and both men ran into the room, "it's there, behind the curtain" she yelled. Walt grabbed a shoe that was nearby, and Mitch slowly pulled back the curtain, they heard the chirp again, and both looked up to the top of the window. There was the tiniest gecko that either of them had ever seen! The resort encouraged the gecko's presence because they managed to take care of other not so friendly critters.

The four of them gathered in the kitchen, to have a quick drink of water after their experience, and laughing, all went back to their respective rooms and settled in for the night.

CHAPTER NINE

FIRST DAY IN PARADISE

The first full day included a little grocery shopping and a lot of pool time. The area around the pool was very tropical, the wind coming off the beach and blowing through the palm and banana leaves made for a nice day. Sweet smelling flowered bushes surrounded the pool and bar area, their natural fragrances mixed with suntan lotion and tropical drinks being served at the swim-up bar added to the atmosphere in a very pleasing fashion.

Mexican music played in the background, mixing with the sounds of the Pacific ocean waves crashing on the bulkhead wall. Later in the day when the tide receded, more of the golden brown sand would be revealed on the beach, inviting courageous swimmers, snorkelers and local fishermen to itself.

While the couples sat under the cabanas, they discussed their plans for the week. Mitch was apprehensive about some of the things that Walt suggested, but they all agreed on swimming with the turtles and having one final dinner at the fancy open-air restaurant located at the far end of town.

Walt looked towards the beach and pointed out the parachute that glided smoothly along the water line, "How about we do that?" he asked the group. Mitch said he wasn't too sure about that but he would consider it.

Mitch mentioned that he and Stephanie would like to do some local shopping and perhaps some site-sightseeing. Walt said they were welcome to it, but he and Penny were all about the resort and the amenities.

Suddenly Walt stood, stripped off his t-shirt and said "Ok Mitch, last one in, is a rotten egg!". The two men ran across the pool deck and jumped into the refreshing water. Walt, always being the more competitive one, said "I win! You buy the next round."

Mitch said, "Too close to call! Double or nothing next time" The two friends laughed and splashed each other. Walt even got close enough to Mitch in an attempt to dunk his head under the water, but Mitch was too fast for him this time, he quickly escaped from Walt's attempt and swam to the edge. He pulled himself out of the water, looked toward Stephanie and cocked his head towards the hot tub.

Stephanie pulled off her swimsuit cover, and met him halfway across the tiled area, hand in hand they departed to the hot tub to enjoy a soak.

On the way to the hot tub, Stephanie looked over and said "Oh! They have an on-site masseuse, that could be fun, if she does couples' massages. A young woman emerged from the salon and greeted her next customer. The sign outside the salon read "Book an hour with Octavia, a once in a lifetime massage experience!"

Mitch glanced at the sign and said "Octavia huh?" "You think her mother was mad when she named her?"

They both laughed, joined lips for a kiss and slid into the hot water.

At the same time, Penny took off her cover-up and joined Walt in the pool, she wrapped her arms around him as he carried her through the water towards the in-pool waterfall, their lips met as they descended under the cool water.

Once inside the cavern area of the waterfall Walt said "I have a few leads on sales tomorrow but we should be able to enjoy most of the day at the resort"

Penny looked at him and said "I know, business comes first, gotta get those tax deductions!". They both laughed, kissed again and emerged from the cavern area back into

the sunlight where the music continued and the blenders
roared.

CHAPTER TEN

THREE DAYS BEFORE THE DISASTER

Mitch, Stephanie, Walt, and Penny all loaded into the pulmonia to begin their vacation adventures. They had called the number on the business card that had been in the gift basket in their room and the driver promptly met them at the front gate of the resort.

They traveled down the cobblestone street to an alley that went between two small restaurants. The road continued under a canopy of a few palm trees and opened up into a neatly raked sandy beach. The driver stopped at the edge of the cobblestone road and the couples exited the vehicle and walked onto the beach.

"Come on Mitch!" Walt shouted as he sprinted through the sand towards the man standing on the beach holding a parachute, connected to an exceptionally long rope which led to a simple motorboat bobbing on the waves of the Pacific Ocean. Walt said that this was a once, maybe twice in a lifetime opportunity but, Mitch was a bit hesitant due to his fear of heights and loss of control. Walt assured him that it was safe, and everything would be fine.

The couples would be parasailing together, Mitch and Stephanie watched as Walt and Penny were raised gently off the beach as the parachute filled with the warm ocean breeze and lifted them into the air. Mitch and Stephanie were next, they were tethered to the rope attached to another boat and were instructed to walk towards the water as their own chutes filled with air. They were gently lifted off the beach and soon were gazing at Mazatlan from a new perspective, a bird's perspective.

The couples were sailing above the ocean, enjoying the warm tropical breezes. Suddenly a drone appeared, first buzzing Walt and Penny, and then Mitch and Stephanie.

Mitch heard a quick clicking sound above the sound of the wind and glanced over to where Walt soared high above the water, he yelled, "I think that drone just took a photo of me!"

Walt yelled back "I think it did of me as well, maybe it is part of the package, a photo remembrance from our experience?" That made sense to Mitch, and he didn't give it another thought until they were safely on the ground and asked the man in charge of the ride about obtaining the photos.

The man said "Photos have never been an option with us, but maybe we should consider it" He assured them that it was probably just a kid screwing around, and not to worry about it.

Mitch said the only thing he would be worried about is if the photos were used to illegally promote another tour or experience and wound up on the internet.

After a short period of recounting their experience, they loaded back in the pulmonia and headed back to the resort for an evening of swimming, dancing by the pool and dinner on the beach.

CHAPTER ELEVEN

TWO DAYS BEFORE THE DISASTER

Swimming with turtles, now this was an activity that Mitch could feel comfortable with. With their history of aquatic adventures, both couples were comfortable using scuba gear, fins, and masks.

The pulmonia driver dropped them off at a dock in the marina area. "Call me when you are back on the boat, and I will come to get you" said the driver.

The boat ride to the reef was about twenty minutes. Once there, the captain of the boat anchored the vessel and instructed them how to enter the water by rocking backwards and falling into the water.

Once the four of them had entered the water, they elegantly glided through the water enjoying the bright colored fish that curiously swam up to their masks and gently nipped on their fingertips anticipating bits of bread. Most tourists paid the additional fifty cents to purchase a snack size plastic bag of bread crumbs to enhance their experience and they were no exception. Everyone enjoyed feeding the fish and watching their reactions as they disappeared into the sea grass and coral and the next wave of hungry fish arrived.

The couples held hands as they glided around the brightly colored corals, sea grass and rocks. The light glinting through the water caused pinpoints of light to flash under the water, almost as if the light originated from the rocky area as opposed to the surface.

Mitch looked over to see Walt and Penny grasping the shell of a turtle and gently gliding through the water. He looked at Stephanie and grasped her hand, they quickly but smoothly swam over to a turtle with a shell with a diameter around 3'. They released each other's hand and placed one hand on the shell of the turtle.

Mitch and Stephanie were surprised how the turtle began moving in a jerky motion. Soon the turtle came to realize that he had a couple hitchhikers and proceeded to guide them through the deep green sea grass to a deeper area in which they were swimming.

They found themselves in a deeper area surrounded by colorful coral and sea grass. Walt and Penny were about 5 feet below them, still being towed by their turtle as if they were being welcomed into the turtle's home.

Many more turtles emerged from rocks, coral and sea grass, swimming and playing around their human guests like they had never known anything different. Baby turtles darted in and out of the rocks, timid about their visitors.

The large turtles slowly came to a stop as if to say "rides over, thank you for visiting". Both couples gave their turtles a friendly stroke down their shells and proceeded to make their way to the surface.

They broke through the water's surface and immediately ripped the scuba masks and snorkels from their mouths and all began talking at the same time. "Can you believe that?" "That was so cool!", "Do you think they always do that?".

Excited chatter recapping their recent adventure made the boat ride back to the dock seem to take no time at all.

The excited conversation continued through dinner as they shared their experiences with other diners at the restaurant.

"What do you have planned for tomorrow?" asked one of the other diners.

"We are planning on a city tour" Mitch said. "I doubt it will be as exciting as today, but still, something we want to do".

CHAPTER TWELVE

ONE DAY BEFORE THE DISASTER

It was another beautiful day in Mazatlan Mexico. Today Mitch and Stephanie were going to go on a tour of the city. Walt and Penny decided to sit this event out and lounge around the pool and beach.

Mitch and Stephanie loaded into the pulmonia and excitedly headed out for a day of adventure.

The first stop on their day tour was the majestic church building located in the heart of the downtown area. Mitch and Stephanie were in awe as they took in the amazing architecture of the building, the brightly colored stained glass windows, the immaculate tile floors and the enormous polished pipes of the organ taking up the entire back wall of the sanctuary.

Mitch jokingly asked Stephanie if there was anything she needed to confess, and she laughed it off saying "Only if we confess together!"

The couple exited the building and were immediately surrounded by children selling gum and candy, they politely said "No, gracias" and placed a single peso coin into their small hands, as soon as those hands had grasped the coin, they were off, yelling in Spanish and approaching the next group of tourist exiting the building.

There was a beautiful arbor just outside the church building and Mitch and Stephanie decided to take a selfie to remind themselves of this moment. A neatly dressed Mexican man stopped and asked if he could take their picture for them, Mitch quickly relinquished his phone to the polite stranger who took several shots of the couple, he returned the phone to Mitch, and Mitch slipped him some peso currency as a thank you for his time.

They found themselves in the pulmonia again and were quickly whisked up a hill to the highest point in the city. From this viewpoint, they could see not only the church building they had just visited, but also the lighthouse on the other side of the bay, the resort, and the restaurant they were planning on dining in the following day. After taking a few more pictures, they headed down the hill. Half-way down, the driver stopped the vehicle to talk to a few locals who were cleaning up a building. While they waited, Mitch looked over, and under the hedge noticed two iguanas chasing each other, the driver took notice and told the couple that he thought that the animals would have to go to confession soon. Everyone laughed and they were soon down the hill and at City level again.

During the rest of the tour the driver pointed out areas of interest such as the lighthouse and the group scrambling up the steep steps on their way to either a wedding ceremony or a quinceanera. Girls with bright colored dresses followed by boys dressed in their Sunday best trudged up the hill, some with their arms full of different packages, either refreshments for the party, or gifts for the guest of honor.

They quickly drove past the local military base, and made their way back downtown. The driver pulled to a stop near the shopping center and Mitch and Stephanie exited the vehicle, they were quickly enveloped with strange sounds and smells, both pleasant and pungent. The couple took some time haggling over a few souvenirs, and after about 30 minutes left the shopping area satisfied with their purchases and with a big hunger.

They asked the driver where they could get some authentic Mexican food, and of course he knew right where to take them. They wound up at a quaint upstairs cafe that overlooked the main street of the City. They enjoyed Sopa de tortilla, rice, beans, and pulled chicken tacos. The food was so good that they were considering changing their plans for the next evening so that Walt and Penny could experience this delicious cuisine.

The driver, who had overheard their conversation, told them that the cafe would be closed the next evening so they would have to keep their current reservations.

Mitch and Stephanie returned to the resort, tired, tummies full and rather euphoric from their day. They went to their room, changed into their bathing suits and went down to find Walt and Penny at the pool.

They found the other couple lounging just outside the poolside bar, their swimsuits were dry, indicating they had not been in the water for quite some time. Mitch and Stephanie recapped their day while Walt and Penny seemed to drink in their stories of fun and adventure as smoothly as they drank their pina colodas.

When asked what they had been up to that day, Walt said "not much, C'mon Mitchie, last one in is a rotten egg" he pulled off his shirt and jumped into the pool, Mitch, not thinking anything strange followed suit.

Soon the two men were splashing each other, racing from one end of the pool to another, and bantering like they had never left the water, and had yet to grow up.

❀❀❀

Earlier that day...

"I don't know why the goods were not up to your expectations, but I will fix this" Walt said into the telephone receiver. "I am on vacation right now but as soon as I get back to the States, I will fix this!" he exclaimed. The party on the other end said "Oh we know where you are, and if you do not fix this error immediately, not only will you not make it back to the United States but there will be a big price to pay. Mark my words agent Brooks!"

Walt hung up the phone, looked at Penny and said "Ready to hit the pool bar?"

CHAPTER THIRTEEN

A FINAL DAY IN PARADISE

The two couples woke up extra early to enjoy their last full day of vacation.

Their day started with breakfast in the little hotel café on the beach. Mitch ordered biscuits and gravy, hash browns and bacon extra crispy. Walt started to give him a bad time about his choices when Penny reminded him that this was their last day of vacation, and he should be nice.

"Yeah, you're right" said Walt just as the waiter placed a large plate of pancakes dripping with sweet syrup and sausage links in front of him. "What?" Walt said, "It's our last full day of vacation, who cares? He said with a smirk.

"Our boys and their appetites." said Stephanie.

It's a good thing they have a good relationship with swimming and working out." added Penny.

They all toasted with their mimosas to a great week full of adventure, and to friendship.

After breakfast, they all agreed they shouldn't go swimming for fear of getting a cramp and decided to take a walk on the beach.

The local vendors had arrived and set up their wares on display for the day. Mitch haggled with a man over some jewelry and wound up buying Stephanie a silver pendant, and he purchased a t-shirt and a hat that said I iguana go back to Mazatlan, a play on the phrase I want to go back.

After browsing the vendor's wares, they continued walking down the beach, the brown sand warmed their feet, and they moved closer to the waterline so they could cool their toes. They came upon a volleyball net that had been erected that morning and decided they wanted to play.

Two other couples joined in and they played a game of four on four. Walt was the first to serve and he sent the ball flying over the net, one of the other teammates easily bumped the ball to the net, while her husband smacked it over the net. Stephanie returned the bump while Penny set the move for Mitch to spike the ball back over. The other couples were not paying close enough attention, and the ball dropped just inbound between them leaving an indentation in the sand.

The game continued, back and forth until the score was 14-14.

It was Mitch's turn to serve, he grasped the ball, bent slightly forward as if getting ready to dive off a podium at the aquatics center, raised up, tossed the ball slightly in the air and hit it with all his might.

The ball soared over the net and came down between two of the other teams' players, one of them barely caught the ball on the tip of her fingers and kept it out of the sand. Her husband, who had been playing next to her reached in and managed to bump the ball a little higher as another of their teammates knocked the ball over the net.

The hand that had met the ball connected so hard that the ball soared over the net and landed out of bounds. Mitch, Stephanie, Walt and Penny had been on pins and needles watching the fiasco on the other side of the net and stared in amazement as the ball soared over their heads.

Game over! They had won the game!

After they had exchanged contact information and said goodbye to their new friends, they began walking back to the resort. They had not realized how far they had walked and it felt as if the sun was beginning to burn their skin. Luckily they had some Aloe Vera in their room.

As they neared the beach entrance Stephanie suggested that she and Mitch take Octavia up on that couple's massage. But first, they stopped by the bar and ordered some water to sooth their parched throats and recover from their impromptu volleyball game.

Walt and Penny decided they were going to hang at the pool for the afternoon but, they all agreed that they would meet their pulmonia driver in front of the resort around 5:00 to go to the open air restaurant and celebrate their final dinner in paradise.

CHAPTER FOURTEEN

FINAL DINNER IN PARADISE

It had been a glorious week in this tropical retreat, and the couples had decided that they would celebrate their final evening in paradise at the quaint open-air restaurant located at the far end of the beach.

Everyone had dressed in their best vacation attire, the men wearing cargo style shorts with button-up Mexican style shirts, a little loose at the neckline. The ladies both opted for skirts and blouses also themed in a Mexican style of colorful stitching, and breathable fabric.

The pulmonia pulled up in front of the restaurant. The restaurant's large door was propped open allowing ample air to flow through the establishment. There was a uniquely carved figure of a Mexican man, with a fishing pole in one hand, what looked like a beer in his other hand, and a handmade "Welcome" sign wedged between his arms signifying that this was a place one could relax and enjoy their time together.

The pulmonia driver said "Enjoy your dinner, call me when you are done and I will come pick you up." He waved to the group, went back to his vehicle, pulled out his phone and punched in some numbers. "Yes, we are here" he said. He then snapped his phone shut, slowly backed out of the driveway and drove back in the direction of the resort.

The foursome walked through the propped open door and were greeted by four waiters dressed in black shoes, black pants, white dress shirts with black bow ties and maroon jackets. The restaurant was obviously freshly mopped, and polished in anticipation of the evening's visitors. They were led to their table past the bar, where the waiter paused and pointed out the custom bar made from a single slab of wood harvested from a *ahuehuete* tree that had grown on the property. The bartenders paused in their drawing of the ice cold drafts and smiled and waved to the couples and said "welcome" in broken English.

They were seated at a table overlooking the cliffs that led to the Pacific Ocean. From there they were able to observe the vendors on the beach walking back and forth selling their wares, they observed some last-minute parasailers gliding over the ocean and took a moment to reflect on the adventurous week they had experienced. Mitch sighed in contentment as they placed their drink orders and chatted about their week.

The drinks were brought to the table, the guys had decided to go with the ice cold beer on tap, while the gals had chosen fruity cocktails with little umbrellas sticking out of them. Walt proposed a toast "to friendship!" he said.

"And the best vacation we have ever had!" added Mitch.

"Vacation of a lifetime!" exclaimed Stephanie. The couples clinked their glasses together, took a long draw on their drinks and looked over the water to see a small plane headed in their general direction.

CHAPTER FIFTEEN

FINGAL

Agent Fingal's fingers glided effortlessly over the keys as he easily controlled the drones and the missiles being aimed at the cozy open air restaurant.

He glanced at the photos taped on the wall. Photos that had been taken over many years verifying the identity of his target as he keyed in the sequence of numbers to detonate the explosive devices attached to the drones.

The first explosion happened in the center of the dining area. Wood cracked, ceiling tiles collapsed on anyone who was unfortunate enough to be underneath them, which included most of the occupants in the restaurant and bar.

The second explosion happened just by the main door, Fingal's idea was to blow the main entrance in the event that his target tried to flee, or the first responders were much quicker than he anticipated, he didn't want to make it an easy recovery mission.

The bartender, totally clueless to what was happening in the next room, until it was too late, dove under the bar, only to be crushed by the weight of the heavy wood as it collapsed. Beer taps hoses were severed and the brew flew freely from their kegs, causing wet and slippery floors in the bar. Waiters rushed to the manager's office to obtain the first aid kit, and to call 9-1-1, but slipped in the foamy mess, lost their traction and either fell and hit their heads, or never regained their footing and wound up stumbling off the edge of the ruined building and fell to the rocks below.

Mitch, Stephanie, Penny and Walt had moved to the edge of the open dining area, and were attempting to climb down to the beach.

Walt yelled to Mitch "I'm sorry man! This is all my fault, they are after me!"

Mitch glanced back and said "What do you mean they are after you?"

Walt said "If you get home before I do, check the safe at my apartment, it will explain everything, again, I am so sor.."

Walt's sentence was cut short as the concussion from the explosion sent he and Penny into the water along with a lot of burning debris and other people.

Mitch and Stephanie had been to the base of the rocks but were also thrown into the water amongst the disaster.

Fingal observed the events unfolding in front of him through the periscope of his sub. "So much for being a weak little boy, what do you think now father" he thought out loud.

❀❀❀

"You are a disgrace to this family!" Yu Jin" "You take nothing seriously, you have failed me!" Fingals father said disgustedly.

"But father, you don't understand, because you are the supreme leader, the people, they treat me differently," Fingal replied.

"You are the son of the supreme leader, you are supposed to be a level above everyone else!" answered his father. "You did not take your admittance into the military serious enough, and now our country is at risk of takeover because I have no one to turn leadership over to"

"I am sorry father, please give me another chance" Fingal replied.

Yu-Jin's statement was cut off at the loud banging on the door to his father's office.

"FINGAL!, We know you are in there, open the door or we will be forced to break it down!" an insurgent yelled. There was a murmur of a group of angry people just outside the door. As the talking got louder, the Fingals knew they were in trouble.

"Go my son, through the passageway" The senior Fingal reached above the fireplace and turned a decorative candle sconce to the right and the bookcase on the other wall started to move. "When you get out of the building, leave the country, save yourself" the older man instructed.

"Father, I shall not leave you, not when this unruly crowd means you harm" Fingal said.

"Just go, before I become more ashamed of you than I am" Fingal's dad said.

Yu Jin ran into the passageway behind the bookshelf which was fully opened now, turned, and took one last look at his father. His father gave him a disgusted look and moved his hand in a sweeping motion indicating that he should go.

Yu Jin ran through the passageway, wound his way around a few corners and came upon a wardrobe next to a door that read exit in Korean.

He opened the wardrobe and found cold weather clothing including a large furry hat, boots, and a warm overcoat. He quickly put these items on and went to the door next to the wardrobe. He slowly opened the door and noticed it led him to a secret area deep in the woods near a waterfall.

Fingal stepped out into the cold air, snow had not yet fallen, but he knew it would any time. He thought back to his father being attacked by the angry mob. He began to feel regret and then remembered the disgust on his father's face and shook it off. "I will prove myself to you, father, just wait and see."

While Yu Jin was contemplating his next move, his father had closed the passageway, poured a shot glass of whiskey, sat on the plush couch next to the fire and waited for the mob to break down the door.

The door splintered, and then broke open, hanging on its hinges. The leader of the mob came into the room and said "Fingal, you are under arrest for the oppression of the people of the country you are supposed to be leading." Fingal took the last swallow of whiskey from the glass, looked up and said "I don't care about the people, they are just the pawns in my ultimate plan."

An obviously strong, bulky man came around the first one that had spoken, a 9 mm pistol in his hand, pointed at Fingal. "Get up, turn around, you're going away to stand trial for your crimes"

Fingal stood, threw his glass into the fireplace, turned around and let the man put handcuffs on him.

Soon after he had arrived in prison, a legal person came, and certified Fingal's signature on the document relinquishing his leadership position.

Yu Jin Fingal took one last look at his observation drone, noted that he did not see any movement coming from any bodies strewn through the building, on the rocks leading to the ocean, or in the bodies floating in the ocean. He directed this final drone to the core of the building and used a self-destruct explosive to ensure that no drone equipment could be identified.

Once Fingal was sure his tracks had been erased, he closed the laptop he had been using to control the attack, ran a quick wipe of the computer's memory and stored the machine to be discarded later in the mighty Pacific Ocean. Fingal then commanded the submarine he was in to dive to 1200 meters so that he could not be seen from any aircraft and attempt to avoid any sonar that he could. Once at its desired depth, the machine was turned west.

CHAPTER SIXTEEN

TREADING WATER

Mitch broke through the surface, spat out a mouthful of salt water and gulped in all the fresh air that he could.

He began treading water while assessing his current situation. The restaurant he and his companions had been in was now just a pile of smoking debris.

Mitch looked over and saw his beloved Stephanie floating, face down in the water about twenty feet from him. He quickly took a few jagged swim strokes towards his wife, flipped her body over in the water and shouted her name. "Stephanie, can you hear me?"

Mitch began to do water CPR, holding Stephanie's nose and blowing into her mouth. After 3 breaths, he turned her head slightly to the side, Stephanie coughed, threw up some salt water, and moaned. Mitch held her head and continued talking to her. "Stephanie, wake up, I need you."

Stephanie's eyes slowly opened, and then closed due to the bright glare from the sun. Mitch used his free hand to shade her eyes, and she opened them again. She slowly broke free of Mitch's grasp, and began to move her arms in a breaststroke motion, treading water.

Mitch had to pinch himself to realize he was not dreaming but he actually was treading water in the mighty Pacific Ocean, looking at his wife treading water beside him wondering what they were supposed to do now.

They couldn't believe what was happening, the dream vacation he and Stephanie had planned and saved for for almost a year (363 days to be exact) had come crashing down around them, literally, within 4 hours.

He vividly recalled the dinner they had shared when they began planning this trip. Now, amidst the debris of wood and fire they saw bodies floating. Bodies of what had been happy hosts and hostesses, bartenders and innocent people who had either been dining at the restaurant or milling around outside. And somewhere in this sea of bodies and debris, his best friend and his wife were floating, but who knew where?

Friends since childhood, he had no idea of Walt's history as a government spy assigned to a foreign country.

Mitch did not know who he could trust.

Mitch treaded water frantically trying to absorb their current situation. "Try to relax," Stephanie said, "if we don't relax, and get our heads right, we will wind up like the other people floating in this mess!"

Looking skyward Mitch realized there was no more air traffic or drones in the area meaning the bomber had done what they intended and were off to collect their bounty on a successful mission.

As he assessed the situation, Mitch saw nothing between them and the shoreline but burning debris and floating bodies. If they could manage to float down about three miles, they could possibly come ashore out of the destruction zone.

As they recalled their past swimming and lifeguard experience Stephanie and he decided to pause from treading water and float on their backs in a feeble attempt to relax and set their minds on reaching the shore. With the tides being enhanced due to the recent full moon, the waves were immense and even if they made it to the shore, they risked getting killed by being thrown into the rocks if they misjudged their arrival point.

As they floated, Mitch gazed at the sky, now a distance from the smoke and flames, the sky was blue with white puffy clouds, a perfect tropical afternoon. He submerged his ears and the sounds of the disaster were muted with the water, adding to the perception of the perfect day. He saw pelicans and terns soaring overhead clueless to their situation, further in the sky he saw the jet stream of an aircraft headed to some foreign land, most likely filled with tourists anxious to start their vacations, businessmen headed to a job or perhaps just people headed back to their homes after spending time abroad.

If only they could see us as well as I can see the pin size airplane, they could radio the coast guard or Mazatlan police, then they would be saved. Mitch knew that no one even knew they were alive and floating in the ocean, they would have to work their way to land or die trying.

CHAPTER SEVENTEEN

CHOOSE SURVIVAL

Mitch awoke to the taste of salt water in his mouth and the sensation of gasping for breath, his body was so physically drained that he had fallen asleep while floating and plotting their arrival on land. Gaining his senses, Mitch looked around and tried to determine how long he had dozed, only a few moments if anything. Mitch and Stephanie glanced in the general direction where their friend's bodies had been lifelessly floating but there was so much debris they could not determine who was who amongst the bodies. They took a few feeble strokes towards the mass of people and debris, got caught up in the swell of a huge wave which projected them towards the beach before they could sort out who was who.

Hand in hand Mitch and Stephanie rode the wave toward the shoreline, Mitch turned his head and looked back to the scene of what had been the quaint restaurant, now a pile of debris and smoke. Sirens could be heard if one listened hard enough, Mexican first responders coming to an unexpected scene.

Mitch couldn't tell if his feet were broken again because of the impact of the explosions, or from being jolted into the water because of the repercussions from the explosion. Deep down he hoped they were only sprained.

They decided to start paddling towards the beach, the sun was setting and the foot traffic on the beach had slowed enough that he calculated their entry onto the shore would be just after dark when the only people around would be either some drunk couples headed to their room for a romantic interlude, or the local sterno bums who called the sand their home.

As darkness overtook them, Mitch and Stephanie paddled towards the shoreline using breaststroke techniques and doggy paddling so as to not draw attention to themselves. The local first responders had managed to put out the fires, threw some floats around the scene to collect what debris they could and the Mexican Coast Guard had removed the bodies of the victims. They had managed to stay hidden a short distance away, clinging to a board that had once been a door or perhaps a bench.

CHAPTER EIGHTEEN

LANDFALL

As Mitch and Stephanie came ashore, Mitch tested his feet, sensitive to the pressure of the sand but not blinding pain as he had experienced years before with broken feet. Only sprained, good news for him as Stephanie knew how to wrap his feet with fabric bandages that would allow him enough support to get to a doctor or at least a medical supply area to obtain the footwear necessary to allow healing to begin.

Mitch drug himself onto the beach and sat facing the ocean while he collected his thoughts. Stephanie crawled out of the water and joined him facing the water. In the distance, the water still lapped and swelled, bringing wooden and plastic debris from the disaster ashore. Any other time this would be a very serene and potentially romantic view.

"What the hell was all that, Mitch? And where are our friends?" Stephanie almost sobbed.

Mitch answered, "Right before that last explosion. Walt basically apologized to me saying this was all his fault" "I don't have all the details, but I think we need to keep our heads down until we find out what the hell is going on!"

The couple rested where they were for about 10 minutes and then heard some voices in the distance, time to move!

Mitch pulled himself to his knees, knee walked over to the seawall and pulled himself to his feet. Stephanie was right beside him and helped him stand. "Are you ok?" she asked.

Mitch experienced enough pain to cause him to curse but did not black out, "My feet are definitely sprained, not broken, some good news right now" he answered.

Mitch limped around the building with Stephanie walking beside him acting as a support. They located a door with a big red cross on it, slipped through the door, located the cabinet with several first aid kits, grabbed 4 rolls of fabric bandage and a bottle of ibuprofen and exited as quickly as they could.

The couple made their way back to the ground floor room as quickly as they could. Mitch had wanted a room upstairs with a view of the ocean, but gave in to Walt's insistence they have ground room floors in case of a fire. With Mitch's sudden foot problem, he was glad he had settled for the ground floor.

Fortunately this resort was older and still used metal keys and not the plastic cards that so many had opted for.

His room key was still in the inside pocket of his shorts. He opened the door, they both slipped inside and went into the bathroom as quickly as his sore feet would allow. Mitch collapsed on the edge of the tub. His feet were throbbing in pain, he dry swallowed 4 ibuprofen and Stephanie set to work wrapping his ankles, very meticulously in the way she had learned the first year in lifeguard training. She had never had to use this technique before, but Mitch was glad she knew what she was doing.

After nearly passing out twice because of the pain, Stephanie had finished tightly wrapping both feet. Mitch limped over to the safe in the room, he opened it, and there was their passports, some extra cash they had set aside and their plane tickets home, They took their belongings and the cash leaving behind Walt and Penny's passports and plane tickets, the local authorities would need some sort of identification to determine who was amongst the remains of the disaster. He deliberately left the safe unlocked and they attempted to get some sleep.

Mitch had a restless night's sleep, being awakened by nightmares and images of planes, fires, and the floating bodies of his best friends. He jumped at every little noise wondering if it was the same people who had been controlling the drones coming to finish off the party. They both awakened early in the day and made contact with the local police. No one seemed to know what had happened to Walt and Penny's bodies and no one was in a big hurry to help them out.

Mitch and Stephanie's flight was scheduled to leave that afternoon and they were determined to get back to the United States as fast as they could and try to sort out what had happened, and find out what was going on.

CHAPTER NINETEEN

HEADING HOME

The flight back to New York was painful for Mitch, he had upgraded to first class in order to extend his legs and elevate his feet, but the cabin pressure was not his friend during this trip. His ankles swelled, and he did not dare take off the shoes that were tied securely on his feet for fear of not getting them back on. He limped his way up the ramp, Stephanie supporting him the best she could. They gathered their luggage and went out to hail a taxi.

Walt had shown Mitch the secret safe in his home several times, only Walt, Penny and Mitch knew about it. Walt had made him promise that if anything ever happened to him he would get into the safe and find the safe deposit box key containing information and tools that would help explain everything. While Mitch had always thought Walt was just being silly. After all, what could a scuba salesman have that was so important?

After being shown the safe, trying the combination several times, including adding Mitch's thumb print, they had had a couple drinks and laughed it off, now the time had come where Mitch felt certain he had to get to Walt's home and to the secret safe containing the key.

Mitch asked the driver to drop him off a block away in case someone was watching for him. He had gone to his home with Stephanie, helped to ensure that things there were safe, and secured the house before heading to Walt's apartment. His feet had somewhat decompressed during the taxi ride, although still painful, he was able to slowly trudge his way to the front door of the apartment building. Because of Walt's mysterious past he had a ground floor apartment.

Mitch reached behind the hallway light fixture, snapped back a little because of the heat from the light but found the extra key that Walt had placed there in case it was ever needed.

Aside from dropping an item off, or picking up something that Walt had asked him to, he had never had a need for it. Mitch pushed the light fixture firmly against the wall and tightened the thumb screw. Just like new.

After using a handkerchief to wipe the light fixture, Mitch inserted the key into the door, unlocked the lock, turned the handle, looked both ways down the hallway quickly went inside, locking the door and the chain behind him.

This time, Mitch put the key on his key ring after entering the apartment, no one would need the extra key ever again.

Mitch worked his way to the hidden safe, punched in the sequence of numbers and scanned his thumbprint. The door popped open, and there was an envelope addressed to Mitch lying on top of the safe contents.

Mitch edged the envelope open and inside printed in Walt's handwriting:

"Hey Buddy! Well, if you are reading this, things didn't bode well for me. I need you to do one last favor for me, you need to contact Sergeant Riley NYPD and let him know that Agent Brooks is officially off duty. Who is Agent Brooks, you may ask? Well, once you find the safe deposit box, you will have some more answers. Do not hesitate, just go! The peace of the country may be determined by your next actions!"

Mitch looked down further in the safe and sure enough there was a key in an envelope marked Republic Bank. There were only two Republic Bank branches in New York, one on 3rd Ave and one on 5th. He would have to take his best guess at which one to try first, but then if he was wrong, the other branch was only two streets away.

The only other thing of interest in the safe was a similar letter addressed to Penny. Mitch thought since they were the only two to know about the safe, that made sense. He took the letter addressed to "My Love" to the living area, found a lighter and ashtray on the coffee table. He burned the letter to ash, dropping it in the ashtray.

Mitch placed the safe deposit box key on his key ring, pocketed the letter, secured the safe back into its hidey hole behind the wedding picture. He then wiped his fingerprints off of the safe, the ashtray, lighter and the door handle. Mitch walked out the door, locked the door with the key, wiped off the outside handle and exited the building.

Moments before Mitch had contacted Sergeant Riley to say Agent Brooks was officially off duty, a small fire broke out in what was Walt's apartment. Fortunately for the contained fire suppression system the fire was contained to just his apartment. Apparently when Mitch left the apartment, a silent alarm had been activated, and without Walt available to remotely disarm it, a sequential series of steps caused the small apartment to be consumed in a matter of minutes, only leaving behind what was left of the contents inside the fire-proof safe.

CHAPTER TWENTY

A MYSTERY BEGINS TO UNRAVEL

Sergeant Riley grasped Mitch's hand as he entered his office. Riley closed the door behind them and said, "I am sorry for your loss, and the country's loss."

Mitch looked him in the eye and said "What the hell is actually going on? What do you know about my friend that I don't, that resulted in me coming back to the states without my friend and his wife?"

Sergeant Riley said, "Coffee? You take one sugar and 2 cream, right?"

Mitch looked perplexed and said "how do you know?"

Riley said, "I know a lot more about you than you realize". "Come with me Mitch, we have some things to talk about."

Mitch followed Riley through a thick metal door, into a soundproof room.

There were photographs covering the wall, not just any photos, but photos of Walt, Penny, Mitch, and Stephanie.

Some of the pictures were from years ago, swimming meets, dinners out, and date nights. Most recently, pictures of the four of them in Mazatlan, parasailing, snorkeling and sitting in the pulmonia taxi that they had taken on their recent city tour.

"Again" demanded Mitch "What the hell is going on?"

Riley sat down, took a long draw on his coffee, lit a cigarette, blew out the smoke exasperatedly and said "Walter, or agent Brooks, has been working for us for a long time, he recently screwed up, and that is why he and his wife are lost and presumed dead."

Mitch looked at the Sergeant, dumbfounded by the last sentence out of his mouth. "Worked for you? Walt was a simple scuba salesman, what do you mean worked for you?"

Riley said "Agent Brooks, I mean Walter has been working undercover for this division of the government since you were both just college graduates. He recently negotiated a deal with North Korea that went bad, and that is why he and Penny are presumed dead."

Riley recapped the conversation that Walt had had with the SEAL recruiter so many years ago.

"So what you are saying is, because I got hurt, Walt decided not to follow his dreams of becoming a SEAL, made a deal with the government to be an undercover spy and, because a deal went South, that he and Penny are dead?" Mitch asked.

Mitch sat down on a ragged couch that looked like it had literally been thrown in the corner of the room, laid his head back and closed his eyes.

A few moments later, Mitch opened his eyes, feeling that everything in the last day had been one bad dream, only, it hadn't been a dream. Yes Walt and Penny were gone, yes he had sprained both his feet and been forced to hurry home, go to Walt's apartment, clear out his safe and report to the NYPD.

A few minutes passed and the heavy door at the back of the room opened, Stephanie walked in, looking confused, but quickly found Mitch on the couch and joined him there.

"How did you know to find your way to the NYPD?" asked Mitch.

Stephanie's voice cracked as she said "They came for me, I was so scared when they came to the house, not knowing who to trust, but I remember Penny telling me that anything happened to her or Walt to go see Riley, NYPD. Those were some of her last words to me ever." she said as she broke down and allowed the tears to fall.

A few moments later, the thick heavy door opened again, and another man came into the room. Riley said "Mitch,

Stephanie, this is agent Thoroughgood. He was in charge of agent Brooks, I mean Walters division."

Thoroughgood strode into the room, extended his arm and shook both of their hands heartily. "I am truly sorry for our loss" he said "you lost a friend, I lost a great agent, Brooks was one-of-a-kind."

Mitch said "Walt was my best friend, I need to know what happened and find out why he is dead."

Stephanie gripped his arm and said "Are you sure?"

"Yes, definitely!" replied Mitch.

Thoroughgood said "I am glad to hear that, because I was trying to find a way to ask for your help."

CHAPTER TWENTY-ONE

A NEW MISSION

The next thing Mitch and Stephanie knew, they were issued new identifications and found themselves on a plane bound for an airstrip in North Korea.

"Won't they know I am not Walt?" asked Mitch?

Thoroughgood said "With as many disguises Agent Brooks wore when dealing with these people, no one knew what he really looked like, except us." "Now what we need from you two is, to get a meeting with this Agent Fingal." "Once you get him to confess that he made the hit on Brooks, I mean Walt, we will come in and apprehend him for war crimes against civilians and make him pay for all the innocent lives he took in Mexico."

"And how am I going to do that?" asked Mitch.

"By making him believe you are Agent Brooks" replied Thoroughgood simply.

❀❀❀

"I don't understand," said Mitch, "Hasn't this Fingal guy talked with Walt"?

"Even if they never met face to face, my voice is very different from his"

Thoroughgood said "We have technology that will change your voice to sound just like Brooks..I mean Walters"

A person dressed in a white lab coat entered the cabin of the plane they were on carrying a rather large syringe. "This contains a computer microchip that will allow your voice to sound like Walt's," the short gray haired technician said.

"But how will I get my voice back when this is over?" asked Mitch.

"We have technology that will enable us to retrieve the chip once this mission is over" said the tech. "Now lay your head back and relax" Mitch laid his head back on the overstuffed headrest of the seat and closed his eyes. Stephanie placed her hand over his and he in turn gripped her fingers, hard. It took less than 3 seconds for the technician to aim the syringe at the base of Mitch's neck, push the plunger and insert the chip.

Mitch wiped the tear from his eye, and said "Well? How do I sound?" Stephanie was taken aback at the sound of Walt's voice coming from Mitch's mouth. The technician adjusted some settings on his laptop and asked Mitch to repeat some phrases until he had calibrated his voice to be an almost identical match to his deceased friend.

The same technician adjusted the wire and earpiece he had equipped Mitch with until they were certain the wire would not be detected and that they could hear everything Mitch could.

Thoroughgood glanced over and said "good, we are ready, fasten your seat belts folks, we are about to land"

Moments before landing, Mitch handed the safe deposit box key to Thoroughgood and said "In case something happens to me, I found this in Walt's apartment but I didn't have a chance to check it out yet". Thoroughgood thanked him and pocketed the key.

"When we land, my crew and I will hang back on the aircraft," Thoroughgood said. "You will ride to Fingal's base with his men, and we will be 5 minutes behind you."

"We have had satellite surveillance on his compound for a while now, it is just over the border in Russia, prime location for someone like Fingal, right on the coast." Thoroughgood said.

"By the time you get Fingal to admit that he was the cause of the disaster, we will be ready to break in and take over the situation", Trust me" concluded Thoroughgood.

❀❀❀

As soon as the plane touched down and taxied to a stop on the tarmac, Mitch and Stephanie deplaned while Thoroughgood and his crew stayed on the plane.

The couple was greeted by one of Fingals men and immediately whisked into a black Cadillac Escalade, with deeply tinted windows. There were two more of Fingal's men already waiting in the vehicle. It was nearly impossible for anyone to see who was in the vehicle let alone see out.

They were quickly driven through the countryside. Just before they entered a wooded area about twenty miles from the airstrip they were blindfolded. "For your own security" one of the men in the vehicle with them said in a broken Russian accent.

They traveled a distance and were stopped at the small coastal border between North Korea and Russia. From what Mitch could guess they traveled about another 35 minutes and the vehicle came to a stop. The couple was led into a building and an elevator.

Mitch's feet were burning at this point, from the pressure of the flight and the change in altitude, he was certainly glad they had been securely wrapped, even though he still carried a cane to support himself.

Mitch counted the dings, and determined they had to be on the 14th floor. Once they were securely in what could be considered a meeting room of some sort, their blindfolds were taken off and they saw they were face to face with Commander Fingal.

Mitch quickly assessed the room they were in. Two doors, one that they had been led in through, and another behind Fingal, obviously a fire escape of some sort. Tall glass windows overlooked a compound area, surrounded by forest land.

Armed guards could be seen patrolling the barbed wire fenced area, some walking with dogs, others with their weapons drawn waiting for someone to breach the fence. Small fires burned in barrels at the corners of the compound. There more officers stood, rifles slung over their shoulders, warming their hands.

CHAPTER TWENTY-TWO

FINGAL'S DEMISE

"Welcome to Slavyanka" Fingal smugly said as he took possession of Mitch's cane. "Or at least the wooded area adjacent to the town."

"We finally meet face-to face, Agent Brooks." Fingal said. "I am surprised to see you...alive. I thought you had been killed in that 'unfortunate mishap' on your dream vacation."

"Tell me, who is your beautiful friend?" Fingal asked.

Mitch replied, "She is none of your business and yes, that 'unfortunate mishap' you speak of actually killed my best friend!" Mitch continued.

"How do you suppose this 'mishap' as you call it happened? And how did you know we would be there?" Mitch asked.

"You are not the one to ask questions here Brooks!" said Fingal angrily. "You are going to be punished for what you did to me!"

"What did I do to you?" asked Mitch.

"You sold me defective goods!" Fingal answered, "But I think you knew that beforehand, which is why you tried to escape to Mexico and drop off the grid. But I am smarter than that Agent Brooks."

"Defective?" asked Mitch, "Defective how? And you haven't answered my other question, how did you know we would be at that restaurant at that time?"

Fingal sighed a deep sigh and answered "Who do you think arranged for your driver?" When I found out where you were going on vacation, I contacted some of the local comrades, and they helped me to make sure you had the appropriate transportation to enjoy your vacation." Fingal said with a smirk.

"The Mexican cartel? Pretty bold for you, Yu Jin" Mitch replied in Walt's voice.

Fingal turned red with anger at the sound of his full name and stammered "The missiles you had delivered to me were defective, they were supposed to be armed with nuclear capabilities, but when received, they were simply surface to air missiles, I could use a rifle and gain the same results."

Mitch asked "Why would you need nuclear capabilities? Are you trying to start World War three Yu Jin?"

"The reason I need those capabilities is none of your concern" Fingal answered. "Now, since you managed to somehow escape that 'mishap' in Mexico, I think it is time for you to pay for your un-business-like actions. You and your companion will both pay for the error".

Mitch replied "I said, leave her out of this, she had nothing to do with any of this."

Fingal answered, "You chose to involve her when you brought her here, to my home and headquarters".

"Now, please have some refreshment while we wait for my men to take you to your new home, far underneath this base. You will like it, it is dark, damp and the ceilings are low enough that you will have to stoop every time you try to stand." Fingal said.

Mitch said, "Before you do that, I have one question. "

"So be it! Ask!" Fingal shouted.

"What about all the innocent people that were killed in the 'mishap'?" He asked, using air quotes when saying the word mishap.

"What about them?" Fingal answered. "Just unfortunate casualties, pawns of the game"

Mitch said "They were innocent people! They had families, lives, jobs, who is going to pay restitution to the families that lost everything because of your officers' actions?"

Fingal paused, looked at Mitch and said "You don't think I could trust one of my officers to do that deed do you? I cannot get my country and my honor back by trusting anyone else with this task, I did that all myself!" Fingal almost shouted.

"My only regret is, I screwed it up by killing the wrong person, it should have been you dead, not your friend, Brooks!"

"So what you are telling me is, you take full responsibility for the killing of innocent people? All in an attempt to gain restitution of an arms deal gone bad?" asked Mitch.

"Yes, Brooks, if you are trying to wear me down and make me say it, I killed all those people in an attempt to get to YOU! And no, I have no regrets about taking innocent people's lives!"

As soon as the words were out of his mouth, Fingal regretted it.

The door to the room burst open, Thoroughgood yelled "Commander Fingal? FBI, International Operations Division. Put your hands where we can see them!" More soldiers burst through the doorway surrounding the trio.

Thoroughgood quickly lowered his weapon and approached Fingal. "You are under arrest for the voluntary manslaughter of over 100 innocent men, women and children in Mazatlan Mexico" He grasped his arms, pulled them behind his back and handcuffed Fingal.

Outside, helicopters could be heard flying over the remote base, spotlights shown on the guards who had been patrolling the fences. Commands to put down their weapons and lie on the ground were repeated in Russian and Korean. The soldiers did as they were told as more armed Mexican and American forces stormed the compound.

A member of the Mexican FBI entered the room in which Fingal, Mitch and Stephanie were. He looked Fingal in the eye and said "You will be extradited back to my country and stand trial for your actions". He then read Fingal his Arrest Protocol, similar to the United States Miranda rights.

Fingal was escorted from the room and into a waiting secured aircraft for his extradition to Mexico.

Mitch asked Thoroughgood "What happens now?" As Stephanie grabbed his cane and returned it to him.

He answered, "Well, Fingal will be taken back to Mexico, probably spend some time in solitary, which I hear is no picnic down there, then eventually stand trial for his actions and be sentenced to death. I hear the trial process in Mexico is slightly behind, so he may wind up spending a few months in a hot dirty cell". "His financial assets will be dissolved, and the money will be sent to the surviving families in Mexico. I know monetary gain does not replace the lives of loved ones, but at least it's something, and maybe the restaurant and surrounding area he destroyed can use some of it to rebuild".

"And what about us"? Stephanie asked.

"The first thing we need to do is get you back to the States, give you your voice back", he gestured to Mitch, "restore your identities and let you live your lives. The lives that should have been lived before Fingal stole it from you. I am truly sorry about your friend, Agent Brooks... I mean Walter" Thoroughgood said, "He was one of a kind, and I am sorry we lost him to our service as well" Thoroughgood added "If he had sold those nuclear capabilities to Fingal, I am sure Fingal would have started world war three, and we would not be where we are today, Walter was a true hero, and will be honored as such."

Sometime later, Mitch and Stephanie found themselves headed back to the States, flying first class this time. The technician had been successful using an electromagnet to retrieve the microchip from Mitch's trachea and he could use his own voice again.

Mitch looked at Stephanie, grabbed his glass of champagne and said "A toast, to my friend Walt, his wife Penny and justice served" They clinked their glasses together, finished their drinks and sank into a deep, much needed and well deserved sleep.

EPILOGUE

It had been a month since Fingal had been arrested and extradited to Mexico to stand trial.

As Thoroughgood had said, it was not a speedy process, and Fingal was slowly rotting away in a jail cell, guarded by local Mexican police, some of whom had responded to the disaster and some that had lost family in the disaster.

In the cell next to him sat the pulmonia driver, arrested for aiding and abetting Fingal.

Thoroughgood, Riley, the Mexican FBI representative and others had called Mitch and Stephanie into the department to personally thank them, and reward them with a new car for their sacrifices.

"On behalf of the United States, Mexico and this division, I would like to thank you for your work on this case Mitch." said agent Thoroughgood.

Mitch turned to Stephanie, looked her in the eyes and said "I couldn't have done it without you"

He glanced over at the photos that had been removed from Fingals compound and pinned on cardboard displays,. Each cluster of photos showed small snippets of their lives, from swimming meets, to picnics, to their final trip to Mazatlan with Walt and Penny.

There were pictures of them parasailing and swimming with turtles, obviously having been taken from either the drones that had buzzed them, or from underwater cameras strategically placed among the rocks in the reef, explaining the bright flashes of light Mitch had seen while snorkeling.

Mitch looked at agent Thoroughgood and said "Can I expect to see any further pictures of our lives from this point forward?"

The agent answered, "No, at this point we have closed this case and you should be able to live your private lives undisturbed by the government."

"*Yeah, right*" thought Mitch as he grasped Stephanie's hand and turned towards the elevators.

Thoroughgood continued "All though, I wouldn't mind if you changed your mind about sticking with the agency, you two make a good team"

Mitch paused, turned back towards Thoroughgood and said "I don't think so, not without Walt. Speaking of Walt, whatever happened with that safe deposit box that I found the key for?"

Thoroughgood answered "Nothing in it but this set of keys" he winked and tossed the keys to Stephanie. He handed an envelope with the title of the vehicle in it to

Mitch. "I figure she's doing the driving until your feet finish healing" Thoroughgood said..

While Mitch believed that there was probably more to the mysterious key and safe deposit box, he let it go, they were dealing with the government after all, and sometimes you are better off not knowing.

As they moved down the hallway, he noticed a rather pudgy man dressed in a green leisure suit with his tie loosened, his partially bald head having a line of sweat running across his forehead, sitting in a chair outside of what looked like an abandoned office. The door to the office opened, and a familiar young lady stepped out.

"Mr. Jones, I am ready for you." said the young masseuse that the division had hired to do on-site massage.

Mr. Jones rose from his seat, and walked towards the office that had been set up with a portable massage table. A pleasant odor of vanilla mixed with lavender wafted through the doorway, and a portable sound machine played a calming classic piano tune mixed with pan flute.

"I am really looking forward to this," he said. "I just hope my time doesn't end too quickly." The masseuse closed the door just as the elevators opened.

Mitch looked at Stephanie and said, "That young lady is very familiar, she really looks like the on-site masseuse they had at the resort in Mazatlan, Octavia, wasn't it?"

"Either twins or a small world" said Stephanie as the elevator door closed and they descended to the ground floor.

The elevator doors opened, Mitch and Stephanie stepped into the bright sunlight, went through the revolving door into the cool outside breeze and walked to their new car, a sporty little coupe with an automatic transmission so Mitch would not have to work his feet so hard with a clutch.

Mitch, always the gentleman, opened the driver's door for Stephanie, skirted around to the passenger door using the hood for balance, looked twice at the surroundings, climbed into the passenger seat and put on his seatbelt.

Stephanie shifted the car into gear, looked at Mitch and said "Where to? The airport? Take another vacation?"

Mitch jutted his chin, looking straight ahead said "Someplace tropical!" Mitch slowly turned his head to look at his beautiful wife, the love of his life that for a brief moment that lasted for an eternity, thought he had lost forever and said, "Let's make sure there is a pool."

Stephanie smiled, turned on the blinker, looked over her shoulder, pressed the accelerator and pulled out of the parking spot with a lurch, leaving the division behind and driving towards their new future.

NOTE FROM THE AUTHOR

Thank you for choosing to read my book *Vacation of a Lifetime*, I really hope you enjoyed the storyline as much as I enjoyed writing it. I hope you feel as if you got to know the characters as more than just names on a page.

I would love to connect with you, find me on Facebook, Twitter, and Instagram and contact me at roscoedonaldson.com.

Look for my new book coming soon. *The Massasin.*

The Massasin

Octavia was just finishing up with a client when she heard a tremendous explosion at the far end of the beach.

"Oh, my goodness, I hope the new friends I met today are ok" Octavia thought as she covered her client with a sheet.

"Doing massage in Mazatlan is unique" she thought to herself, "You don't need any heat on the table, and the clients are usually more relaxed than normal, so the job isn't nearly as difficult as in other areas."

Suddenly her phone buzzed, she looked at the number and said to her client "I am truly sorry, I have to take this, but I will give you extra time, relax, I'll be right back."

Octavia stepped out of the salon and quickly answered her relentlessly buzzing phone. "I'm just finishing up with a client, make it quick" she whispered into the phone.

There was a pause, and Octavia sighed, "I'm on vacation for another 3 weeks, and then I have some other jobs lined up, Yes, I have a client right now, I worked a deal with this resort to make a little cash on the side" she explained.

"Fine, I understand, I will be back in the States in about a month" she said sounding exasperated.

As she clicked off her phone, she looked up the beach and saw smoke coming from the quaint restaurant, she said a silent prayer for her friends and went back into the salon.

"A few more bonus minutes and your time is up" she said.

The client sighed a deep sigh and said, "that was a fast hour, your sign is correct, this is a once in a lifetime massage, thank you Octavia."